A SHADOWLAND OF THE SURREAL

REVISITED

Alien Contact Experiences

GEORGE SYRING, Ph.D.

ISBN 978-1-959895-39-8 (paperback)
ISBN 978-1-959895-38-1 (ebook)

Printed in the United States of America

THIS BOOK IS DEDICATED
TO MY MOTHER AND FATHER
IN LOVING MEMORY

CONTENTS

PROLOGUE

The professor gave me graded papers and requested I return them to the students in my English class. D plus appeared prominently on the first paper which was written by me. I wondered what the purpose was of putting a plus after his alarming D. It made no sense and seemed like some slightly sarcastic icing on a mini cupcake. The D indicated what my writing was worth. Sweeping rather swiftly through the text, an interesting issue immediately emerged. Anything about aliens he crossed out in red ink. I was so surprised someone in an academic atmosphere could not accept aliens around us. Then the dream departed before becoming completely conscious.

My subconscious mind wanted to make plain that alien denial really disturbs me. Denial turned out to be the basic trouble with my first contact book and was hard to handle. I am just like everyone else except there is no problem being with aliens. My mind finally made me face reality and realize I am not just like everyone else.

I have lived a double life **among** aliens as a hybridized human being. They consider me one of them genetically and provide complete medical care without cost plus abduction protection. These aliens have come here from a far-away planet in the Andromeda Galaxy over 2.5 million light years beyond Earth. They are endowed with incredible powers impossible to imagine.

This alien material no doubt is disturbing and may appear more like fiction than fact. Spaceships are not "psychological aberrations" as endorsed by expects but fantastic alien flying machines fully armed with advanced weapons. They have been a part of my life from a babe in arms. Little three-fingered gray friends sometimes invite me to fly with them like Superman. I have seen the Earth looming large above a lunar landscape from inside an alien moon base. Mars has a highly advanced subterranean civilization. Already as a kid, aliens started taking me there to play with several special Martian boys my age. We grew up together and remain friends. Alien genes allow me to talk telepathically. Individuals from twelve separate alien groups have been in contact. Officials overtly contend no contact has happened. My hybrid alien grandson Jon is so unique in part because he is also my deceased hybrid son Jon. Details follow in the first chapter on Jon.

Many minds always are completely closed about aliens. Everything true in this book is bound to be beyond belief for some folks. An old timer once approached me in the local post office and asked if I really wrote a book on aliens. I said yes and offered to give him a copy. He refused it because there are no aliens. His mind did not want to be confused by facts. Aliens never exist among those who never believe they exist. A copy of my work was sent to someone in another state. She called and wondered how it was possible to write a book on aliens There is nothing in the Bible about them and she reads it every day. Bro. Brimstones are very apt to agree with her. Several locals said they never bothered to finish reading the books I gave them. Something either was difficult or impossible to believe and probably both. At least hybrids enjoyed the book and never were a bit bothered by anything alien. Take advantage of this opportunity to open your mind and be in resonance with the reality which surrounds us.

Now is the time to admit an alien presence already prevails among humans. Footprints it leaves are increasing rapidly as aliens continue weaving control ever more tightly into the fabric of our existence. When their plans for this planet finally are activated, a radical new reality will result while the world as we know it comes to an end.

CHAPTER 1

JON

I said the conscious mind of my deceased hybrid son Jon decided to be recycled for whatever reason in the Finale chapter of my first book on alien contact. No doubt he gave me all the details on December 21, 2014, when his mind came to visit me for the last time. Our conversation was blocked so I had no idea what was discussed. I found out he was recycled on February 4, 2015, when my mind suddenly received two photos on that date from his alien friends on another planet who were watching over him.

Some small security service spaceship seemed so low when I walked outside one evening in February of 2015. I went back inside and printed a note with my black magic marker. Once again outside, the message was shown to the ship. It read, MY DEAD SON. TELL ME WHAT HAPPENED. PLEASE. I hoped a reply soon would follow. The guys responded, but not in a way I was expecting.

At the end of February 2015, my little dog Sugar and I returned home from our usual morning walk. Early that afternoon I could not account for an hour of missing time from 11:00 AM to noon. I finally figured out what happened. Some of Jon's security friends I know came to visit with me. They told the details about how Jon was recycled. Then these guys blocked my memory before departing. I ended up learning nothing and became very frustrated. That was on top of the 40 minutes Jon spent with me in 2014 near Christmas. It finally began to dawn on me Jon was recycled in a most unusual way. I wondered what it could be. My other hybrid son came to visit me four months to the day after Jon was recycled. If he told me something about Jon, it was blocked. More than two years passed before I finally heard about Jon and was allowed to remember it.

I was getting ready for bed on May 10, 2017, when someone spoke a single sentence to me by nonverbal mental telepathy. Supplying words to that sentence he said, Jon was recycled into the body of his infant son. Jon is now the conscious mind of his own son he named Jon. He is my son and my grandson. I am his father and grandfather. He is a hybrid of a hybrid and probably one of a kind. He wanted to be genetically a part of his brother and me. Jon is now seven years old and in school with his friends.

I talked with my doctor years ago about hybrids and their ability to reproduce. He said it is not possible. Mules are hybrids and cannot produce mules. No wonder everyone including Jon did not want me to learn how he was being recycled. There was considerable doubt he would live past infancy. Chances were slim to none and slim already left town. Jon is a hybrid miracle child. After 27 months, alien doctors decided he was going to live. It was then I was told about Jon for the first time. Never once had I thought about being a grandfather. Now I am so happy to be one. Sometimes it seems impossible to imagine this little boy's conscious mind once lived inside my brain as the conscious mind of his deceased father Jon.

CHAPTER 2

SURPRISES

The sky already was dark enough to see a couple lighted spaceships on patrol above us as Sugar and I were coming home from our evening walk. We stopped to watch them on Cypress Drive where it intersects with my unpaved subdivision road. I waved to them, and they responded by flashing their lights. They obviously were from the local alien base and recognized me. We continued our walk home.

The following morning an SUV from the base was coming north rather rapidly on FM 1120 while Sugar and I slowly walked south. I knew what they wanted. My geography class at the base was supposed to meet again at any time now. They would expect me to wave consent to be picked up at night by a tractor beam of light from a spaceship projected through the roof into my bedroom while asleep. This time though something very surprising happened. The vehicle suddenly slowed down to a crawl as it approached us.

Up close this black vehicle looked disturbing. It was freshly washed and shiny as usual, but all windows including even the windshield were tinted black. Those seated inside were not visible. There was a look of evil about it. As a quick aside, I found out later aliens know how to make vehicle interiors look black so clear windows appear tinted from the outside. In any event, the slow speed suggested something sinister. Fear quickly consumed me, and visions of Men in Black entered my mind. I was known to them, and they were coming after me. Waving was not what would happen.

I hoped this episode would blow over, but it was just the beginning. No matter where I took the dog for our morning walk a car would follow and expect me to wave. A variety of different cars appeared, and I wondered where they found them. One dude even drove up beside me with his window rolled down trying to intimidate me. They were getting desperate now as I refused to wave. The following paragraph comes from the Farewell chapter of my first contact book and sums up the conclusion to this entire affair.

Things went downhill rapidly in just a couple weeks. Jon was not around to help me. I was starting to be concerned for my safety by the time Jon appeared. He sent me a short mental film clip of his response to the situation. He knocked the base commander flat on his back with a single blow to the abdomen and then relieved him of his command.

Several days after his film clip, Jon came to see me at home during the night. He wanted to take me back to the subterranean base, so I went along with him. My geography students were waiting in our classroom. Everything I said to them was blocked from my memory, but the very first sentence came through the block several nights later. I thought I never would see you again was the sentence.

Jon died on June 25, 2012, from severe injuries he suffered in a single car accident. Some of his friends in security tried to tell me about his death. They mentally projected a film of us in class after he brought me back to be with these students. I saw and heard myself say I thought I never would see you again. That really amazed me. Too much attention was paid to me and not enough to Jon. I wanted to see the film of us together one last time after I realized Jon was dead. All my interest now was focused on Jon.

There was no doubt about it. Jon and I were genetically father and son I said in the Shocks chapter of my first book. That chapter was emotionally trying to write, and I wanted to hurry through it without dredging up details. I let readers assume we looked alike, so he was my son. The truth is his appearance was a shock. He looked nothing like me. Anyone seeing us together never would suspect a family relationship. I knew we were father and son because his face was a carbon copy of my mother's face. She was alive again appearing now as her hybrid grandson Jon groomed in casual men's clothing. Jon and I were father and son. There was no doubt about it.

CHAPTER 3

MEN IN BLACK

Most of what we know about the Men in Black comes from individuals who were in contact with them and talked about their experiences. Stories follow a familiar pattern in much the same way as experiencers detailing their abductions.

Everyone contacted by Men in Black has one thing in common; they all have seen UFOs during the day or night. Contact began during the early 1950's when spaceships suddenly made themselves manifest much more frequently. The grays were gearing up their hybrid breeding program for full-scale production and wanted to keep it secret from the public. They decided their best bet would be to intimidate observers by using Men in Black to thoroughly threaten them into keeping quiet. These guys always knew whom to contact and where to find them.

The men arrived in an old black sedan that instantly appeared and disappeared. After knocking on the front door and it opened, they invited themselves inside. All were dressed in a similar manner wearing a black suit and classic black fedora hat. The few photos I have seen of them taken in public places show rather dreary faces that remind me of mortuary employees. I dread to think these guys might show up at my front door one day and welcome themselves inside. Maybe they have been told not to contact me.

Speculation has been rampant that the federal government maintains its own Men in Black program. No one with access to freedom of information documents ever has found evidence of them. The problem is government workers never could gain access to the detailed information the grays had on individual observers who were remaining quiet and never went public. In any event, it seems highly unlikely there is any federal program in existence today.

I always have suspected Men in Black are hybrid humans rather than robots as some ufologists suggested. Eventually though I changed my mind. These guys appeared just when the hybrid breeding program was gearing up and there were no adult hybrids to intimidate spaceship observers. Aliens had to settle for robots. Their strangely similar appearance and artificial intelligence seem to indicate they rolled off some sort of alien assembly line.

Several years ago, I read two separate accounts of women in England who invited a MiB inside their homes. One woman in the first story saw an electric wire running along the leg of her visitor when he sat down. I just could not believe it was true. The other woman offered her guest

a drink and he had no idea what to do with it. That makes sense for a robot who never needs to eat or drink.

The third and most recent account comes from YouTube. A fella had to deal with two MiB individuals who invited themselves inside after he opened the living room door. They proceeded into the kitchen and asked whether the microwave oven was working. The homeowner said no. The next time they appeared and walked into the kitchen, one of them pulled the plug from a wall outlet. The impact of microwave radiation on their electronic components evidently was a major concern. During his conversation with these guys, the house owner revealed he was moving and did not know the address of his new home so they could not find him again. One of them replied, "We can find anyone." I describe how this is possible in the next chapter.

A most disturbing MiB film clip recently was shown on YouTube. A hidden camera filmed all the action inside some local business reception area. A MiB walks inside and approaches the receptionist sitting at a desk behind the counter. No audio of their conversation is provided. The young woman suddenly pulls out a gun from a drawer and points it at the visitor. What happens next is most interesting. She puts down the gun, walks around the counter and disappears out the front door with the MiB. She disappeared permanently according to a voice in the film. This was a most incredible display of robot mind control. I suspect it might be the first time MiB mind control has been filmed. Perhaps aliens have upgraded their robots.

Mind control. You may know the expression without experiencing it. Aliens can make anyone do what they

want without any verbal or nonverbal command. Response is automatic with no thought of resistance. We become marionettes dancing to the tunes they play so to speak. I have danced many times to their tunes.

CHAPTER 4

THEY KNOW YOU

I said aliens know you in the Living with Jon chapter of my first book. Anyone with even a limited amount of common sense must have thought likely story. That just is not possible.

Early in my alien literature reading, I came across an abduction experience of some guy in the U.S. He believed aliens know everyone on this planet. Sometime later I read about an abducted woman in Europe. She believed everyone in every country is known to the aliens. This time I paid attention to her.

Years later a hybrid friend at the local alien base showed me a long computer list of names arranged in alphabetical order. I quickly looked down the list, and the only name familiar to me was mine. Information of all kinds appeared after each name. I was stunned. Never once had it crossed my mind material about me appeared on file in some alien computer. I am aware now and the implications are most disturbing. My thoughts drifted back to the individuals in the literature who were certain aliens know everyone, and I had to believe they were correct.

Aliens know who we are and where we live. Perhaps you wonder how they can keep track of us. I have known for years but never told anyone. Recently a guy here in the U.S. said he was told during an abduction. What a surprise an alien let the cat out of the bag. No telling whether it was a mistake or intentional. In any event, now that the public has been made aware, I feel safe in saying they can locate us by tracking the brain wave pattern of every individual. Each person has a unique brain wave pattern just like fingerprints. Our patterns are kept on file in a computer for easy access in tracking someone.

Suppose you see a lighted spaceship while outside at night. Your identity is safe from scanning because aliens cannot see you in the dark. Truth be told, you appear on a monitor as if in bright sunlight. They record your brain wave pattern and match it with the same pattern stored in a computer. Almost instantly they know who is watching them, where you reside and all about any pertinent poop. If Men in Black are told to intimidate you about a sighting, they can track down your location without any problem.

Aliens also can track someone with a brain implant through the nose or right ear. It is a painless but bloody procedure done usually at home during the night. I describe how accurately they can keep track of me in the First Anniversary chapter of me previous book. The precision literally can be down to an inch. In that chapter I also say, other alien groups can tell quickly to whom I belong.

That was written well before I realized what a problem my implant would pose for me. Hybrid military officers now need to maintain 24/7 observation to prevent an attempted abduction.

This chapter surely must seem like so much science fiction. Alien technology is advanced beyond ours by light years. In a very real sense, they come from the future to be here in the past with us.

CHAPTER 5

TIME

Aliens live in a different world than we do when it comes to time. We segment time into past, present, and future. The present is where we live. They occupy all three segments at once. Time is continuous with them, and they can move forward or backward without any problem. When they move backward, people now deceased are very much alive. They say no one ever dies for this reason. My hybrid son Jon moved into the future and saw he died at an early age because of injuries in a single care accident and prepared to live with me as a conscious mind after his death. People involved in remote viewing can do the same thing as aliens. It's a skill anyone can learn. Psychics do something similar when they see into the future and describe their visions.

There is a significant difference between past and future. The past is carved in stone and cannot be changed. Although the future already exists, it is subject to change made by actions in the present. Psychics who make wrong predictions about the future probably saw it before changes happened.

Several years ago, I read an article written by a photographer who was employed by the Air Force to take pictures inside a small, abandoned spaceship. An officer told him to come outside after 15 minutes. He went inside and realized the interior was the size of a football field. He could not understand how that was possible. Aliens can shrink exterior sizes of ships without diminishing interior dimensions. After 15 minutes, he walked out of the ship. A clock showed the correct time was 6 hours later then the time on his watch. Time inside moved much slower than time outside. Hybrids never wear a watch because they can see the correct time mentally. Strangely enough, their mental time is one minute faster than our atomic clock time.

Scientists who back engineered a crashed spaceship near Roswell, New Mexico, in 1947 discovered it was a time machine. Many aliens are time travelers rather than space travelers. They come back here to the past from the future. The Invitation chapter of my first book describes a story of aliens who said they can come back here no matter how far away their travels take them in 10 seconds. These guys go faster than the speed of light which our experts say is impossible. This kind of sun revolves around the Earth mentality is what keeps us so far behind the curve in spaceship propulsion technology.

You probably know little or nothing about time reversal and never have experienced it. This ability used to be unique to the aliens, but the Secret Space Program uses it now to return crew members to the time when they first joined the program 20 years earlier. In any event, aliens can move people from the present to the future and then return them later to the past which is now the present. For example, they lift me out of bed at night and take me somewhere for a month. Then I am returned to bed 15 minutes later in the past which now becomes the present for me. Because my memory of the experience was blocked, I wake up in the morning without knowing what happened. The Mars section of the Joe chapter covers time reversal in more detail. I often have experienced time reversal making me older than my present age.

CHAPTER 6

FLYING

The setting sun seemed surprisingly large as our spaceship landed in a rural area of an inhabited twin planet between the Earth and Venus in an invisible dimension of the solar system. A group of little gray flying friends wanted to show me something they thought would be of interest. The ship parked miles away from the destination for some reason. The distance was too great to walk so we flew there like Superman only our arms rested beside us instead of extending straight out in front. I enjoyed the view of a mostly level landscape passing underneath us. If you have an interest, more information about this planet called Terra appears in two chapters of my first contact book including a visit there in the Cosmic View chapter.

A flying partner to the right suddenly caught my attention. He was looking at me but not in the same way I was looking at him. I knew from experience he was gathering data on my vital signs and making sure all systems were working well. They always were checking on the status of my health. Everyone thinks exactly alike so my health data are shared equally among them. When I talk to one individual, all of them hear me. When one of them talks to me, they all talk to me. I never have been able to decide whether these guys are sentient beings or robots with highly advanced artificial intelligence. It would not surprise me if somehow, they were a hybrid combination of the two perhaps in a manner like Men in Black.

They do not carry weapons while flying, but concern for my safety never has been a problem. Any threat they can handle with their collective minds. These guys know how to keep all kinds of guns from firing. More sophisticated weapons like lasers they instantly can figure out how to block or disengage.

We arrived at our destination after a short flight. What they showed me originally was blocked from my mind, but the block disappeared after my first book was published. The guys took me inside one of several buildings constructed by an alien civilization that occupied their planet thousands of years ago. A black and white picture in a black frame hung on a back wall. My guess is it was placed there recently as a tourist attraction. In any event, the picture was a profile view of an alien apparently associated with the building. He had a bird face like a raptor while his body looked entirely human. The bird was bald except for a clump of dark feathers extending along and above each side of his head. I would call this alien an avian humanoid.

Months later I accidently came across a profile view of this same individual in the computer painted in color on the tomb wall of some Egyptian several thousand years before now. He must have been a person of importance to be painted on the wall. I am willing to go out on a limb and say this may be the only painting in existence of the aliens who helped the Egyptians build the pyramids. See the Nefertiti section of the Joe chapter and read for yourself what aliens have to say about construction of the Egyptian pyramids.

By the time we were ready to fly back to our ship, the level of light was getting dim at dusk. No little guys surrounded me as usual once in flight, and I wondered what happened to them. With my head turned back to the right as far as possible, I saw them clustered tightly behind me. They were flying blind. There was not enough light left for them to see with their black eye covers. I knew then why they put me at the head of the pack to lead them back to the ship. Their confidence in my flying ability was surprising although they had no other choice.

Until now there never was any need for me to make flying decisions. The guys were in control. I just went along for the ride. Once control passed to me, I became responsible for the safety of everyone. Movements were managed by merely thinking about them; for example, going higher or lower and slower or faster. Flying partners, mind reading my thoughts, made every move for me. This extraordinary experience seemed extremely exhilarating. A fading afterglow became apparent and alarming while vacant land below looked black as pitch. I was flying blindly for all practical purposes with no star or moon light visible in a clear night sky. Then our parked ship appeared suddenly ahead of us. Bright white light, reflecting from such a shiny metal surface, served so successfully as a brilliant directional beacon. My flying friends finally brought us back down with a smooth landing by the ship. To be onboard once again was a relief.

Much to my surprise, hardly any accounts are available about flying with the little grays in the alien literature. My guess is only hybridized humans are selected to fly with them and almost always memories are blocked.

Janet Bergmark has had some interesting experiences while flying alone. In one of them, she suddenly comes up against a tall building along her flight path. Instead of a fatal impact, her body passes right through the structure. Once the outer wall is penetrated, building materials like insulation, plumbing, and wiring pass by her. Several other individuals have told some similar stories about their flying experiences.

Budd Hopkins describes in detail the abduction of a young woman in New York City. She lived on the upper level of a tall apartment building and was taken right through her closed bedroom window by two little gray aliens into the night air. Many people observed her flying with them over the East River to a spaceship hanging high in the sky. Traffic on the Brooklyn Bridge came to a halt as everyone watched the spectacle of her flying. Even a United Nations official on the bridge saw her through the window of his limousine. Flying with the little grays is real and not imaginary. How it works no one knows. All I can say from experience is it takes two of these guys, one of each side, to lift me into the air.

Another form of alien movement besides flying concludes this chapter. I know nothing about how it works, but perhaps this will become a future form of locomotion for us. What I am talking about is a jump room. The name is misleading because no jumping is involved. What happens is we go from point A to point B without passing through the distance between them. Going through the atmosphere or outer space is not involved. Movement takes place in seconds. Let me give you some idea of how it works. Suppose I want to go to Mars. I walk into a tightly sealed chamber. The entry door is shut and locked. Several seconds later the door is unlocked and opens. I walk out on Mars. What would have taken me seven months travel time by a modern spaceship took only several seconds. In a very real sense, jump rooms work much the same way as alien telepathic machines discussed in Chapter 11. You know now aliens know how to move in moments over millions of miles.

Chapter 7

TELEPATHY

Experts agree mental telepathy is an actual ability although how it works is not known.

In the Conversing with Jon chapter of my first book I say, Jon and I were talking together for quite some time before it occurred to me, we were communicating mentally. It was a surprise to realize I had the ability.

Several people I know say they talk telepathically to aliens in their spaceships after dark. None can hear me say something to them by mental telepathy. They also claim aliens talk to them. When I tell them some confabulation the aliens told me, they report aliens said the same thing to them several days later. All of which shows without any doubt both parties to a telepathic conversation need to have the same ability.

Some researchers believe it is only a matter of time until telepathy is taught to everyone. I doubt it. Hybrid children can talk telepathically without being taught. They were born with the ability. Without any alien genetic material in them, no one can learn telepathy. Aliens never would have given me some of their genes if they knew I could be taught to talk telepathically.

A commonly accepted opinion today is our brain controls mental telepathy. All we need to do is find where the ability is located and activate it. Experience convinces me the brain has nothing to do with telepathy. A life-long friend came to visit me early one morning. He died 25 months earlier so his brain was long gone. He was a ball of light and we talked telepathically. He came to say goodbye and was leaving to be recycled by the aliens into a newly born infant. They told him I am one of them.

Telepathy is associated with the conscious mind rather than the brain. After my hybrid son Jon died and his conscious mind came to live with me, we talked by mental telepathy. He even had all his alien bells and whistles with him. Hybrid friends often put me into a state of suspended animation and remove my conscious mind so they can talk to me or take my mind with them. Welcome Home and The Invitation chapters of my first book have some details. We will not understand telepathy until the conscious mind is understood.

Gradually I began to realize it is possible to speak out loud to someone with a telepathic ability and still be heard no matter far apart we are. I also can be heard perfectly by mixing mental telepathy with speech. The conscious mind can hear every word regardless of how we speak with one another. If I am talking telepathically to someone and my thoughts suddenly drift from the conversation, the listener can hear everything I am thinking. You can imagine how embarrassing this can be. Concentration on the conversation is essential in mental telepathy.

I have no mind reading ability like the aliens and hybrids. From the Mental Visitors chapter of my first book I say, they feel it is perfectly acceptable to enter my mind and help themselves to whatever information they want. Like vultures, they have stripped clean the carcass. More recently, however, I have come to appreciate their mental contacts. If I have a problem, they quickly know about it and come to help me.

I do have some ability which is a sudden awareness or "higher knowledge" as someone in the alien literature called it. Those of us who have the ability usually are associated with aliens in some way such as an abduction. Quite often I know something about individuals meeting me for the first time. A good example of my ability is a recent experience.

My pickup and I were headed down to the local post office. We were waiting on Cypress Drive for a car to pass by at the intersection with FM 1120. I decided the car belonged to no one I know as it approached. The interior was too dark to see the driver as it finally passed us. I suddenly knew the driver was a woman and she was headed for the post office. There was no doubt about it. When I turned into the post office parking lot, her car already was parked facing the building. Once I walked inside, the only person there was an unfamiliar woman standing beside her open mailbox. I have no idea why my conscious mind became aware of this useless bit of information.

Hybrids read the minds of one another. This must be an effective behavior control tool. They have no need for our expensive and elaborate criminal justice system. Guilt or innocence is determined quickly by mind reading. The guilty go directly to prison for punishment. Their prisons are more like short stay motels than our long-term care facilities. Prisoners are tortured and allowed to leave prison soon after their injuries have healed. Mind control may be something to look forward to in a future world dominated by aliens.

CHAPTER 8

HYPNOSIS

What we know about gray alien abductions comes primarily from hypnotic regressions. Most conscious minds are deliberately blocked during an abduction. Hardly anyone is permitted to remember the experience. That is why researchers use hypnosis to gain access to the subconscious mind. One problem is people sometimes lie deliberately while under hypnosis. Another concern is whether people are influenced to say what hypnotists want them to reveal. For this reason, there is some question whether hypnosis is a valid research tool.

Three alien abduction researchers who have used hypnosis professionally are Budd Hopkin, Dr. David Jacobs, and Dr. John Mack. Hopkins pioneered the use of hypnosis on abduction experiencers. Then he trained Dr. Jacobs in his hypnosis methods. They worked closely for many years and the results of their research are quite similar.

Hopkins realized early on abductees were telling quite similar stories although none of them knew one another or were familiar with alien literature. Tales of terrible emotional, mental, and physical abuse were common. Individuals often had implants inserted into various parts of their bodies. Some experiencers were abducted repeatedly to harvest ova and sperm. Both researchers have written most disturbing books about the results of their research.

Dr. Mack then started to make public the results of his own abduction research using hypnosis. The experiencers with whom he worked were treated very well by the aliens. No one was used or abused. Then word leaked out Dr. Mack was favorably disposed to the grays. The conclusion was obvious to everyone. He deliberately led those under hypnosis to say favorable things he wanted to hear. The limitation of hypnosis as an alien research tool was becoming apparent. Hopkins and Dr. Jacobs disliked the grays, so they had bad results.

Years later I came across the book written by Dr. Mack with transcripts of his hypnosis sessions. I quickly paged through it and read several complete transcripts. What amazed me was how objective and professional he was. No evidence appeared he deliberately led anyone to make comments favorable about the grays. I was most impressed with him.

Why did his results differ so significantly from those of the other two researchers? I found out Dr. Mack was very selective in his choice of those with whom he wanted to work. He apparently used some sort of criteria in the selection process but what it was I could not determine. It dawned on me finally why the results of Dr. Mack were so far out of line with those of Hopkins and Dr. Jacobs.

Without realizing what was happening in his selection process, Dr. Mack ended up working with hybridized human experiencers. The grays never would abuse anyone genetically a part of them. No wonder so many had such pleasant experiences to relate under hypnosis. Hopkins and Dr. Jacobs worked with anyone who needed help. Their experiencers were little more than laboratory animals. The grays could care less how badly they mistreated and mutilated them.

Gray aliens arrived on Earth long ago with the intention of gaining control of this planet. Hybrid breeding played a key role in their plans. These guys realized disturbing stories about their abduction practices would surface very soon in the news. They needed someone of substantial stature who would refute all allegations.

No doubt the grays knew Dr. Mack very well as someone they hybridized with a good deal of their own intelligence genes. He had a brilliant mind which opened many doors for him including head of the Harvard University medical school. Aliens worked on his conscious mind and got him interested in doing abduction research using hypnosis. They made sure he selected other hybridized humans as subjects for hypnosis who had wonderful things to talk about the grays. No wonder his research results were substantially at odds with work done by Hopkins and Dr. Jacobs. Fortunately, no time was left for him to hear about his plight as an alien set up victim due to a sudden and surprising accidental death according to authorities.

CHAPTER 9

UFOLOGY

Dictionaries define ufology as a study of UFOs. Most certainly UFOs are not studied like history or math at the college and university level. Tons of information have been collected and stored, but rarely does anyone bother to study the material. It would be wrong to consider ufology a field of study in my opinion.

It is a field of interest in UFOs largely populated by people with an unknown level of education and intellect who come from a broad range of backgrounds. Some interested individuals like to make themselves seem singularly significant by collecting sighting information. Relying entirely on outside observations for understanding the alien enigma is rather useless. No wonder ufology has reached a definite dead end. Only when individuals with inside information and alien contacts come forward will there be a badly needed breakthrough in ufology.

Very few ufology experts report having an ongoing relationship with aliens. Not one of them claims a telepathic ability. Beneath this top level of experts are investigators with years of experience gathering information on the alien phenomenon. At the bottom of the pyramid are considerable numbers of people with alien interests including some sheep-shearing speakers showing up at various UFO gatherings.

Corey Goode, Barbara Lamb, and Bob Dean are three members of this elite expert group I have selected for special consideration. All of them are exceptional human beings with personalities that lend themselves well to an alien association. No wonder individuals from different alien groups have chosen them for contact. You do not hear their names mentioned on the nightly news, but quietly they have made the most monumental news of this century by revealing aliens known to them are among us.

Corey Goode has managed to capture the minds and imaginations of everyone interested in ufology to an extent that is unprecedented. He was a member of the Secret Space Program financed by black budget money as an intuitive empath communicating with extraterrestrial beings as well as interfacing with alien federations and councils among some of the positions he held. He also is aware of the Solar Warden program which is said to have 10 unified combat commands with antigravity vehicles the size of aircraft carriers that operate only in outer space. His own web site is easy to access if you want to know more about him and his alien activities. Revelations he has made along with others sporting similar backgrounds are mind blowing to say the least. We are way more advanced than what NASA and the pentagon are willing to admit in public.

Barbara Lamb is a regression therapist, researcher, speaker, and author of books on the alien enigma. I have watched some of her lectures on YouTube given at UFO conferences. She is an excellent speaker with a wide range of knowledge about aliens. Some alien contacts are considered friends. Barbara Lamb is a national treasure who deserves the highest award possible for her contributions to the field of ufology.

Bob Dean was a retired U.S. Army officer and a ufologist living in Tucson at the time of his death at the age of 89 in 2018. He first became aware of aliens while in the military after reading a classified document called "The Assessment" that described threats posed by alien beings on Earth. He appeared on radio talk shows, TV programs and UFO conferences where he talked about government cover up of the alien phenomenon. He grew up along the Ohio River across from my hometown of Cincinnati.

Ufologists who have received wide recognition for the quality of their research are Richard Dolan, Linda Moulton Howe, and David Wilcock. All of them are featured quite frequently on YouTube. They have spent decades acquiring an extensive knowledge of the alien enigma. They speak with authority on various topics at conferences, seminars, and workshops as well as radio talk shows including interviews. Linda Moulton Howe made a name for herself with cattle mutilation investigations. David Wilcock recently joined forces with Corey Goode in a partnership that ought to be advantageous for both guys. These individuals have managed to turn their expertise into cash cows and must be doing quite well.

Experts at this second level are outsiders who have no alien contacts for inside information. They rely on second-hand information from questionable experiencers and alien literature making them dependent upon often unverifiable material that may not have any basis in fact. This brings up a final thought I have which concerns a present and pressing ufology problem.

It is plagued by a lot of nonsense based on greed, ignorance, and stupidity. Unlike astronomy where scientists write professional papers published for peer review, all kinds of amateurs write articles that never are reviewed by professionals before they are published. As a result, anyone interested in the alien phenomenon is bombarded with confusing or completely worthless information that is totally at odds with reality. The following titles are good examples such as The World is Flat, Aliens are Demons from other Dimensions, The Grays no Longer are on Earth and Extraterrestrials are Artificial Intelligence. Folks who feed on false material like this have a mindset that is difficult to deal with and nearly impossible to correct.

CHAPTER 10

DEBUNKING

Sightings of UFOs have been reported for decades. All sorts of objects have been used to account for what people were seeing including airplanes, birds, weather balloons and even swamp gas. Photos of UFOs were discounted as trick photography. Physical evidence from UFOs examined by experts was explained away as junk or a hoax. Debunkers managed to discredit almost everything presented as alien evidence out of fear or ignorance.

Phillip Klass was very widely recognized as the single most visible and vocal debunker during his day. A charitable chap of indefinite intellect once described him as a "UFO skeptic." Far from being a skeptic, this deliberately disbelieving debunker seemed set on some special messianic mission to decisively discredit all convincing alien evidence. His completely closed mind managed to attract several strong supporters along with a fully-fledged fanatic fringe of fruits, flakes, and nuts. He had no use for ufology and worked diligently to destroy it. This guy was heard singing frequently from the same sheets of music as government debunkers. Whether his name appeared on some secret payroll as a federally funded debunker remains unknown. When disclosure debases debunking, Phillip Klass will be declared a fraud and his imprint on ufology forever forgotten.

Debunking of UFOs became government policy in 1947 with the crash of an alien spaceship outside Roswell, New Mexico. Military officers at the crash site described some details, but government officials quickly changed the story to a downed weather balloon. Aliens and their ships were unknown back in those early days so officials hoped the public would accept the balloon story. So much was concealed and hushed up that even today ufologists find it frustrating to piece the puzzle together.

Most likely the Roswell incident led to a 1947 decision by President Truman to create a secret committee of scientists, military officers, and government officials to recover and investigate alien spaceships. This committee was referred to as Majestic 12. The government had some concern that social order would collapse if the truth about aliens ever became public knowledge. Tightly controlled news media were pressured to reveal little if anything about UFOs and alien abductions. This policy worked well for the grays who were concerned about concealing their hybrid breeding practices.

Dr. David Bennewitz, a businessman and brilliant electrical engineer, probably was the most prominent target for government debunking. He lived north of Albuquerque, New Mexico, and used some sophisticated radio equipment to intercept transmissions between spaceships and a subterranean base in the Archuleta Mesa near Dulce, New Mexico. The base was a joint venture between the government and aliens. He was disturbed by all the human rights violations going on there and unfortunately brought attention to himself by going public with what he knew. Expert government debunkers quickly attacked him with so much false information about aliens at the base he had a complete mental breakdown. Whistle blowers working at the base finally began to reveal much of what was going on there. Stories they told were mind blowing and beyond belief. For those of you who know nothing about the Dulce base, let me give you a brief description.

The base consisted of seven levels below the surface. The top level was used for security and communication. The next level down was for humans and staff housing. Executives and labs occupied the third level. Mind control experiments were on level four. Aliens were housed on level five. Genetic experiments were carried out on level six. Cryogenic storage occupied all of level seven. This seems like a rather regular research facility where nothing out of the ordinary happens until you dig much deeper for details.

Thousands of abducted U.S. citizens were brought here and kept in cages at the deeper levels or placed in cold storage. Human beings were used as lab animals or abused in genetic and mind control experiments. Other humans were raised like livestock and kept as a food source for reptile aliens. Some individuals were eaten alive. Chemical changes in the meat caused by pain and terror made the flesh taste better. Human body parts also were kept in huge storage vats full of liquid for the reptiles to eat. Genetic experiments were horrific. Humans were produced with multiple arms and legs or were used for genetic cross breeding with animals. They might produce a pig with a human head for example. I realize it sounds sick and beyond belief, but all this is true. Perhaps you can understand now why the government went all out to debunk Dr. Bennewitz. They could not permit him to go public with the truth about activities at their Dulce base that had to be kept secret from scrutiny. Government financial support for such a scandal most surely would stop.

Military officials quickly followed in the footsteps of the government with their own debunking program. When I was growing up, the story was aliens never bothered the military. Officers were kept in the dark about the serious alien situation. I believed what I read until one story after another finally began to surface about plane crashes due to alien military action. Quite a few planes were lost, but the crashes always were attributed to accidents of one kind or another. No one was the wiser. This shows how effective debunking and intimidation of military personnel worked to conceal the truth from them.

Some military officers recently revealed to Congress and the news media that alien spaceships have appeared at nuclear missile installations. More than just appearing, they managed to figure out the entire missile launching sequence and how to stop it which means they can prevent missiles from being fired. Stories from Russia and China also have emerged about the same situation. In June 2017, a captain in the Air Force revealed 10 missiles inside launch silos were destroyed by alien UFOs. The military hushed up the attack. Hard telling whether there is anything of substance to support this story.

Government debunking efforts to the contrary, interest in all things alien has started gaining speed due in part to ufologists who have publicly promoted their research results. Now the pentagon suddenly has shifted its story which seems to signal some significant change in sentiment. My guess is this UFO/alien enigma will break wide open and people finally are forced to face the terrible truth that was denied for decades. The shock is bound to be well beyond endurance for many closed minds clinging desperately to denial and delusion about aliens among us.

CHAPTER 11

CONTACT

Astronomers suddenly receive some complex radio waves on their radio telescope arrays that repeat once more and then disappear. Local interference is suspected at first. Wave pattern analysis rules out any stray signals. Further examination confirms the signals come from 250 light years away. Someone in the neighborhood is broadcasting an intelligent message. No one can make any sense of it. Then a computer expert discovers the signals form a photo of the senders. These guys appear humanoid rather than human. Mainstream media manage to obtain a photocopy for worldwide distribution. The shock is enormous even for alien believers. No longer are we alone in the cosmos. Talk soon surfaces of an alien invasion. Physicists crawl out of the woodwork and assure everyone invasion is not possible for 250 years if these aliens can travel at the speed of light. There is no need to worry about an invasion. Before you believe this explanation by experts, let me share some sobering news with y'all. Highly advanced aliens really do occupy a planet 250 light years away and say they can be here in 5 minutes. Most likely these guys are time travelers who arrive here 5 minutes before they left home by going faster than the speed of light back into the past.

Radio telescopes appear to be our best bet for alien contact. Dr. Seth Shostak at the S.E.T.I. Institute says he is confident contact is going to happen in just "a couple decades." I am not surprised he said that with his position to protect. Astronomy is outside my area of expertise, but I do have inside access to aliens who can answer my astronomy questions They made me aware radio telescopes are not very well suited for cosmic contact.

The problem is radio waves traveling at the speed of light are way too slow for contact over galactic distances. Instant contact is possible for aliens without any transmission involved regardless of the distance. If this sounds impossible, you are not up to speed with alien technology. Our scientifically sophisticated cosmic companions use artificial intelligence machines designed to duplicate human telepathic ability. What one machine thinks another one knows instantly many light years away. We have no ability to intercept this kind of communication. Once telepathic machines replace archaic radio telescopes, we will be able to access the galactic communication network and make all kinds of cosmic contacts.

Dr. Enrico Fermi wondered about our lack of alien contact way back in 1950 over lunch at the National Laboratory in New Mexico. He said there are billions of stars with planets surrounding them, yet no one has contacted us.

He asked where everyone is or are we alone in the cosmos. The problem became known as the Fermi Paradox. Academic experts and nonprofessionals alike have tried to resolve this paradox without any agreement after 70 years.

The difficulty with the Fermi Paradox is it reflects an anthropocentric point of view that does not dovetail well with thinking by highly advanced aliens. My individual alien contacts certainly convince me they know all about us but have no intention of making formal contact. Even our neighbors on Mars stay so silent. Those who want to believe we are alone in the cosmos either are incredibly ignorant or unfortunately unrealistic and probably both.

A more important problem now is what constitutes a convincing alien contact. Scientists want nothing less than verifiable proof at the highest government level. An alien delegation standing next to their spaceship shaking hands with the President on the white house lawn surely would satisfy them. Contact by radio telescope with civilizations light years away also is easy to verify. Do not hold your breath for either type of contact. They will not happen anytime soon.

Sometimes I wonder if people who count on contact ever consider the consequences. It would be like the outside world meeting a primitive tribe isolated in the Amazon rainforest. As with them, our way of life will likely collapse. Limitless energy replaces present energy production. Organized religions rapidly disappear. Money-based economies are apt to be replaced by barter or something entirely new. Advanced alien civilizations no doubt realize the problems and have no desire to deal with them.

Physical contact could pose immense problems. Diseases might be transmitted from them to us resulting in multiple pandemics for which we have no cure. If they talk only by mental telepathy, communication could be extremely difficult. Repulsive and/or terrifying appearances surely would create emotional problems unless they are able to shape shift into human form. Invasion might be their real **motive for making contact. In other words, cans of worms could open that cannot be closed.**

Some aliens including those from other dimensions, who are curious about us, move on to greener pastures once they realize we have not advanced far enough for travel faster than the speed of light. Local galaxy inhabitants less than 500 light years away come to see what new toys the neighborhood kids are playing with now. Visitors sometimes contact individuals in whom they have an interest. Reptile aliens once selected me for abduction and contact. The Dream chapter of my first book has the details. Mental contact is much more frequent than abduction. Pleiadeans, for example, suddenly started contacting me one evening by projecting photos into my conscious mind.

Pleiadeans are a race of alien humans from the Pleiades' star cluster some 420 light years beyond Earth in the Taurus constellation. Their technology is much more advanced than ours. They talk a lot about joy, love, and peace. Their reputation is probably the highest among all the alien races in contact with us.

During the summer of 2018, a Pleiadean made mental contact early one evening. He projected a photo that consisted to three separate parts. I can recall only the middle and bottom parts now. The middle part was several lines of strange writing. The section below was a pencil drawing of the sender who had long stringy shoulder length hair.

The next time he sent a single photo. It said, "I AM A PLEIDADIAN" in white print on a black background. Now I finally knew who was in contact with me.

The third time he sent a painting of a beautiful young girl. I recognized the style of painting as typically Pheidian from photos that appeared in YouTube. The painting was mainly in blue. I told him by mental telepathy I did not like paintings with so much blue. He then sent a painting of a young girl in yellow and bright colors. I said these girls were not familiar to me and I would like to see some photos of his planet as a geographer.

His first photo was the branch of a flowering fruit tree with blossoms like those of a cherry tree only the color was a spectacular deep purple rather than pink. The second photo was a sunset with a lot of red and purple in the sky. The last photo consisted of a group of small buildings with flat rooves taken from a high elevation. It looked like a desert setting with no green vegetation. These photos were interesting but not what I had in mind. They obviously had no intention of showing me anything of geographic interest. I began to wonder why they bothered to contacted me.

A woman in the neighborhood who read my first book sent me an email that was a long list of topics to be presented at a big Pleiadean public event. I read through the subjects and realized there was a common thread running through all of them. It was mind control in very subtle ways. This listing read like a deceptive ploy some religious cult might use to attract unsuspecting prospects. Then a program appeared in YouTube about Pleiadean mind control. I never bothered to watch it, but another individual also came to the same conclusion about them.

I let my hybrid military friend know of the Pleiadean contacts and said I wanted to stop them. His mind entered mine to verify their photos and mental copies left with him. Photos suddenly stopped. I was amazed how quickly the military had communicated with the Pleiadeans. Something probably was said about dire consequences if contact continued. My alien friend told me later they "threatened them." Once dust finally settled, the ending seemed sad. This guy was pleasant and tried so hard to accommodate me. He projected a final farewell film waving goodbye from his car window. No time was left to thank him or even ask his name.

Investigate before you invest is some sage stock market advice. The same advice certainly holds true before investing your mind with the Pleiadeans. Information of all kinds is available about them through the internet. Much of it is produced by the Pleiadeans themselves. Do not be swayed by their paintings of lovely ladies who probably never even existed except in the minds of the artists. These guys are great at altering the truth and creating realities to fit their needs. Mental manipulation is the price you pay for associating with them. Contact is certainly for their benefit rather than yours. Remain very wary of the Pleiadeans.

It was the dead of night. I went walking down a dark and stark city street when some dude approached me wearing all black apparel. A black hood concealed his facial features. He intended to interrogate me, but his speech was impossible to interpret. It seemed unusually high pitched and sounded like so many screeching birds. I panicked and screamed. He disappeared instantly as I began to wake up in bed.

This was the first time an alien attempted to contact me through my subconscious mind. I was too inexperienced and emotionally unprepared to cope with it. No one ever tried to teach me how to handle alien contact. I learned from experience to remain cool, calm, and collected enough to interact successfully with anyone regardless of the appearance.

Every sentence in this paragraph about the man in the mask comes from the Day Visitors chapter of my first book. He had on his black mask, but suddenly his right hand grabbed it at the top and removed it. I had braced myself for a horrific sight when he pulled off the mask. He said he had been in an accident. His facial features, except for his eyes, were burned black beyond recognition. The next thing I knew he was standing next to me, and we were shaking hands. His fingers and hands were surprisingly large and powerful. He certainly appeared humanoid but not human. He continued to hold my hand as we talked, and his hand was very warm. He did most of the talking and I did most of the listening. He got me home safe and sound.

I knew this experience was most peculiar, but the purpose never occurred to me until after my contact book was published. It was a test. Aliens wanted to see how I would react. They have put me through similar tests all my life. There were three parts to this test. The first one simply was seeing an alien wearing a mask. I could cope with it. The next part was removing the mask and showing me his charred face. There was no way I could scream and wake up in bed this time. We were inside an alien satellite station under his control far beyond the moon in outer space. Now I needed to concentrate on dealing with it. Previous contacts provided enough preparation to handle such a sight without showing any slight emotion. In the third part, we shook hands and talked telepathically with one another. His English seemed perfect and without an accent. He was a nice guy and a pleasure to meet. The aliens found out what they wanted to know, and probably I passed their test.

Some friendly guy from Mars currently is in mental contact with me. More information about my life among Martians appears in the Mars section of Chapter 12.

There also is another human male who contacts me from a planet in some solar system like ours within the galaxy. He has transmitted photos of himself and his family along with printed texts in English. Everyone looks Caucasian, and no one would pay any attention to them in a public place like Walmart as they dress just like us. I thought they were from our planet at first until he sent a picture of a small table model globe of his planet.

Several interesting geographic observations about the planet immediately became apparent. It is a land planet without oceans or large bodies of water. No high mountain ranges were obvious. There is a striking surface similarity to Mars at such a small scale. Photos taken outside his home show a nicely landscaped yard with green grass and tall broadleaf trees in the background. The climate in this area must be either like Humid Subtropical or Humid Continental. Both polar areas lack a large ice sheet, showing his planet is located closer to the sun than Earth in a habitable zone. At the north pole an enormous hole exists several hundred miles in diameter. It looks as if a huge crustal chunk collapsed into a **cavernous chasm. The edges of this abyss are jagged rather than smooth suggesting** the opening might be continually expanding. Taking a tour of his planet and visiting with him while there would be wonderful.

A contact is covered next that may seem surprising since I am now the alien who meets humans on their planet during an out-of-body experience. What immediately attracted my attention was the sun. I appeared high above me and looked like an enormous red ball that produced a low-level of light like that seen on Earth as an afterglow. The air temperature was warm enough for everyone to wear summer clothing which made me wonder how that was possible in such a dim light.

My sight suddenly shifted to nearby parked cars. They were not extremely futuristic looking as expected. All were vintage model vehicles dating back to the beginning of the 1940's or earlier. My dad bought a brand-new Studebaker in 1940 for $700 that looked more modern than some of them. Seeing these cars again brought back childhood memories of life during World War Two. I soon discovered their level of development was at least 80 years behind us. I had not gone back in time though because their sun was not right, and they spoke only by nonverbal telepathy.

A young guy maybe in this middle 20's, who served as my guide, introduced me to a select group of individuals waiting to greet their visitor. Although no one spoke English, that did not pose a problem. They read my thoughts and responded by nonverbal telepathy which I understood. No doubt they selected me for contact due to my telepathic ability and experience among aliens. Their voices and language never were heard as we stood there talking in total silence. The encounter was like speaking with aliens on Earth only I typically talk to them telepathically in English and they speak by nonverbal telepathy. These folks were so kind and a joy to meet.

My guide and I ended up at a local restaurant. A waitress adjusted our table so we could sit at right angles to one another and talk. The dining area appeared almost empty, so this was not mealtime. Suddenly I woke up bed and decided to revisit the experience mentally one more time.

This was not a typical OOB experience. My alien guide arrived at home during the night and abducted my conscious mind once he placed me in suspended animation. We went to his planet at the speed of thought. The whole procedure was reversed after returning home. I cover a similar situation in the Welcome Home chapter of my first contact book.

Plenty of time has elapsed to examine my experience. Speculation sure seems easy, but getting it right is difficult. My dad used to say I am good at putting 2 plus 2 together and getting 22. The intention here is to do better as I try to put pieces together, so they make some sort of sense.

What seems safe to say is this planet I visited revolves around a red dwarf star in the habitable zone. After reading a good deal of detailed material about Proxima B, my conclusion is this is some other exoplanet that remains to be detected. The star, however, likely appears in some astronomical catalog.

Perhaps these people hold a key to explaining their failure to progress as we did after World War Two. Several members of the group I met had severely deformed faces or heads or both. It broke my heart to look at such wonderful individuals who were so kind and glad to meet with me. I have come to some very tentative conclusions about their plight.

My best guess is these human beings never evolved naturally on this planet. Their ancestors originated on some other planet like Earth and were abducted by gray aliens who brought them here for some specific purpose. The entire population has remained very small resulting in a reduced gene pool which led to mutations as people started interbreeding. This small colony has managed to survive on food and supplies provided by the grays. Cars dating back to around 1940 reflect the time aliens settled the planet with humans. They never have provided updated models. The only escape for these people has been limited to out-of-body experiences on other planets including Earth. They must have some alien genetic material in them since they can talk telepathically and saw me as a sentient being. I wonder if the grays told them about me and the locals arranged a meeting.

There is another possibility I want to present that could account for some surprises seen on this planet. It concerns gray alien hybrid breeding practices. There have been two different programs and I am a product of the first effort which ended sometime around 1941. They created hybrids then by harvesting ova and sperm from humans already containing alien genes. The process was long and slow resulting in a small number of hybrid births. Alien officials applied pressure to produce a greater volume at higher speed on the order of an assembly line production. Experts exerted every effort to perfect a procedure that permitted use of ova and sperm from anyone and adding their own genetically engineered material. Soon after starting this second phase of production something most surprising went wrong. Disturbing physical defects were detected in hybrid infants. By the time all production wrinkles were ironed out, a substantial number of badly deformed children existed. Grays have a reverence for life and refused to euthanize them. The situation was solved when the grays found a planet where the children could be shipped for special care. Nothing more is known. My OOB experience could have happened on this planet, and I met with some offspring of original children. A limited gene pool explanation might be dead wrong. Perhaps I put 2 plus 2 together and got 22. If my conclusions fail to find favor with you, have no hesitation to present your paper featuring new facts found from recent research relevant to this topic.

Everyone expects contact to come when aliens show up suddenly in spaceships or intelligent signals are received by radio telescopes. While we wait and wonder which will come first, aliens already are visiting us out-of-body and making mental contact. The remainder of this chapter concludes with a few of my own experiences.

Many years ago, my mother and I were doing dishes after dinner when she suddenly said something about her OOB experiences. They started as a young girl at home and continued until recently when she decided to stop having them. Her experiences were such a surprise and most interesting to hear. I decided to divulge nothing about mine, but apparently my ability was acquired from her.

I have had OOB experiences on other planets for quite a while. Some of them have been on inhabited planets in parallel universes according to aliens. They have raised my vibration level so I can function perfectly on planets in higher dimensions. There are times when I am gone so long my body goes into something like hibernation. It feels refrigerated and I need to pull up blankets during the summer to get warm. Several of my experiences might make most entertaining reading. None of them will be published to prevent anyone from asserting I surreptitiously substituted sensational science fiction fantasies for facts. When truth is told beyond toleration, rabid ridicule results. Perhaps that problem is precluded now.

The great advantage of OOB experiences is travel time totally disappears. Some scientists say distances are so vast interstellar travel on spaceships never may be possible. Truth be told OOB traffic is tremendous between planets. These guys are invisible allowing them to go anywhere and see anything they want. No wonder our planet is known so well throughout the cosmos.

Aliens frequently project color films and slides into my mind while awake in bed. Someone sends a slide show on the 14th of every month that concludes with a redbud tree in bloom as his sign. This fella is familiar to me, and I have been on his planet. Most aliens are anonymous. Someone recently sent slides of his planet taken from high in the sky. I opened my eyes and watched the show progress on a white bedroom ceiling that served so successfully as a projection screen. There were no large bodies of water. A lot of land areas appeared covered by green vegetation including peninsulas and islands surrounded by rivers. No cultural features like buildings or cities appeared which is done deliberately. A couple weeks ago a single slide appeared of a flower garden in bloom full of day lilies with maroon petals and yellow centers. The sight was spectacular. Flowers are featured fairly frequently, and many seem so special they must be native to other planets.

A slide show suddenly appeared just after shutting my eyes and attempting to take a nap after lunch on July 20, 2022. Every photo was in color, and each lasted only a second or two before the next one arrived. Timing was too swift to see any details, but various landscape views were the subject matter of most photos. Only two slides lasted long enough to examine the contents.

The first one was an urban area street map that looked exactly like a typical city map in this country. Streets were positioned as parallel straight lines that intersected at right angles forming a familiar grid pattern. I concluded they have modern urban centers with paved streets able to accommodate a substantial flow of vehicular traffic. Various types of land use must exist on the blocks between streets. We might feel right at home there unless buildings are so architecturally advanced, they appear out of this world.

The second photo featured the face of a male who perhaps was active in putting together this show and then projected it into my conscious mind. Light was dimmed down making it deliberately difficult to discern his facial features. I sensed he seemed like a simian alien character with short black hair that covered his entire face and head. Being brutally blunt though the appearance looked remarkably like sasquatch photographed all around our planet. An old saying goes you cannot tell a book by its cover. That might be an apt adage for this fella. I have managed to meet with several wonderful aliens whose countenance could create considerable anxiety for anyone seeing them. The real puzzle remains how do aliens acquire information about me and what motivates them to initiate contact. I may have met them once upon a time during an OOB experience.

The main takeaway I hope folks have from this chapter is an astute awareness aliens already are active among and around us. We are not alone in the universe and never have been. As this age of academic indifference about aliens appears ending, another amazing age of alien contact absolutely is approaching. Resolve to Resonate with Reality!

CHAPTER 12

JOE

Spaceships protect me night and day from abduction regardless of the weather. They appear at night in the east and disappear in the west just like star movement. One ship, however, moved from north to south. I could watch the lighted ship pass from left to right across my bedroom windows while lying in bed. I would get up sometimes and signal hello to the pilot with my flashlight and frequently he responded by flashing his lights.

Near the end of October 2017, I went to a window and flashed my light to say goodbye. He would be leaving soon with the change of command and crew on November 1. Never again would I be in contact with him. Much to my surprise, he flashed all kinds of colorful lights. For the first time, I talked to him by mental telepathy. I asked if he read my recent book concerning alien contact and his response was yes by flashing lights extremely fast. I spoke to him every night until the end of October when he disappeared. One night in early December he appeared suddenly again. We continued our contacts. I told him I would call him Joe and he flashed his approval.

Joe began projecting photos of himself into my mind along with other subjects of interest. He is a Native American hybrid named Lonewolf. His appearance is like Sean Connery as James Bond only even better looking and much more muscular with body builder biceps. Some who see him for the first time must have my place or yours on their minds. Joe is a great example of alien genetic engineering. One photo showed him in a military uniform with decorations.

Christmas was approaching and he started sending me all kinds of beautiful Christmas photos mentally. Several Christmas cards looked unique as if they had been made especially for me. I want to share one of them with you. The card consisted of two diagonal lines coming to a point forming an abstract Christmas tree.

The tree was black. Not very appealing, but there is more. Bright colored lights the size of pin heads packed the entire tree. Every little light was blinking in such a way that not even two of them were in unison. It was an incredibly beautiful display of twinkling lights that only an alien artist could create. Another card was a tall Christmas tree full of fabulous ornaments with white electric lights. The sight seemed so spectacular. He made it a Christmas to remember.

Time was running out near the end of April 2018. Crew and command changes were scheduled for April 30. Joe would be leaving, and that would be the end of him for sure. He must have gotten a papal dispensation to return after leaving in November. Pressure was building and I decided to ask Joe if he were willing to be one of my hybrid family members. I was so surprised and tremendously thrilled when he said yes. Then I asked if he would mind looking after my grandson Jon and he agreed. The change came and went but Joe has remained to watch over me ever since then and is my best friend.

Joe has been a tremendous source of information on a variety of topics. I have asked him questions on subjects of interest to me. Perhaps they might attract your attention as well. While reading through the rest of this chapter, keep in mind his responses reflect remarkable alien knowledge which can diverge considerably from contents in mainstream media news.

Coronavirus

By now everyone knows the virus originated in Wuhan, China, and became a pandemic. The question was whether it originated from an infected animal or resulted from a laboratory accident outside Wuhan. Numerous specialists said they had hard evidence it occurred naturally while British experts announced an accident was responsible. As the pandemic became more severe, news media lost interest in how it started. I asked Joe if a laboratory accident accounts for the problem, and he said yes.

When vaccines became available, I never bothered to ask Joe about having the injections. At my advanced age surely, he would say yes. Then I changed my mind and decided to seek his opinion. Both times I asked he said no. My guess is alien doctors told him to say no should I enquire. Joe told me at the beginning of this pandemic their doctors have a drug that kills the virus. I decided to avoid all vaccine injections and visit a doctor at the local alien base when the virus is detected in me.

Dr. John Mack

Joe confirmed he was the victim of an alien setup. A car hit and killed Dr. Mack while he was crossing a street in London, England. No doubt the aliens were aware of his fate and made sure to get all they wanted from him before he came to a bad end.

Insectoids

These guys are highly advance alien insects that look very similar to a praying mantis only they are several feet tall. I have read they originated on a planet populated entirely by various kinds of insects. They must the dinosaurs of their insect world. Very often these insects are seen on spaceships with the grays during an abduction. Dr. David Jacobs feels certain these insects created the grays and are in control of them. I heard Barbara Lamb say she knows a woman who is a product of insectoid hybridization. She looks entirely human but holds her arms in the same praying position as the insects. I asked Joe if he ever met these alien insects and he said yes. Then I asked if these alien insects created and control the grays. He said no.

Multiple or Parallel Universes

Scientists including astronomers and astrophysicists are starting to speculate our universe is finite and other universes exist beyond this one. Aliens say an endless number of universes stretches to infinity. Some universes have a complete lack of life. I asked Joe if parallel universes exist. He said yes.

Ukraine

After Russia invaded the Ukraine on February 24, 2022, I told Joe one night the Ukrainians sure needed some alien support and asked if they were willing provide it. No response was evident. That did not surprise me. Hybrid aliens help only those they consider one of them.

Websites on YouTube recently have featured films and stories of divine intervention in Ukraine. One film showed columns of bright light extending down to the ground from dark clouds. They obviously were tractor light beams projected from invisible spaceships. Another film featured a bright light in a cloudy night sky followed by a group of Russian soldiers unable to fire their weapons in the morning. Aliens know how to prevent every kind of weapon from working. They also can prevent missiles from firing or fail to explode on impact. Our government reports a 20 to 60 percent failure rate for Russian missiles. Were these signs of divine intervention or acts of alien involvement?

I was wide-awake in bed talking to Joe by mental telepathy around 2:00 AM as Central Daylight Time approached on March 13, 2022. Rather than watching time change, my interest was centered on those YouTube films of divine intervention. I decided to ask him if hybrid military officers really were supplying some direct assistance. He was reading my mind and said yes before the question could be asked. I was so happy to hear these guys were giving a helping hand. No telling who made the final decision to intercede, but certainly Joe used his considerable influence to get approval. Faithful folks never will believe their divine interventions were acts of alien involvement by hybrid military men.

Phoenix

A U.S. city reporting the greatest number of UFO sightings is Phoenix, Arizona. A spectacular display of lighted UFOs occurred there one night during 1997. Known as the Phoenix Lights, they were seen by thousands of residents and photographed extensively. Officials attributed them to flares set off by Air Force officers in an unbelievable attempt at debunking. I asked Joe if these spaceships are coming to visit Phoenix, Arizona, from a city called Phoenix on a planet named Terra located between Earth and Venus in an invisible dimension of the solar system. He said yes without any hesitation.

My alien tour group on Terra, consisting of several humanoids and a single human, arrived in Phoenix during a hot summer afternoon with an air temperature around 120 degrees Fahrenheit or even higher. I realized quickly why they named this city Phoenix. Like their sister city in Arizona, it is situated in an area of arid climate. The main difference is no natural vegetation grows there including xerophytic plants like cacti giving the site a lunar landscape appearance. Beautiful buildings beyond imagination lack lovely landscaping. Gray desert soil surrounds them that looks like poured concrete pavement. Perhaps they have some water supply problem and need to practice conservation. The entire planet is warmer than Earth with no polar ice caps due to its location closer to the sun than Earth. Additional geographic details about the city and planet appear in my first contact book if interested.

Do not be concerned about residents of Phoenix visiting in Arizona. They hardly are malevolent alien monsters but highly intelligent hybridized human beings who look like us and speak perfect English without an accent. I would not be surprised if they shuttle between Phoenix and their sister city in much the same way residents of Alaska shuttle between Anchorage and Seattle. They probably shop at Big Box stores like Walmart, Lowes, and Home Depot. Some individuals even may live and work among local city residents. Lighted spaceships appearing frequently in the night sky are just a tip of the iceberg so to speak. Formal contact seems certain in the future with residents of both cities visiting one another by traveling back and forth on spaceships equipped to pass between different dimensions.

Jeffrey Epstein

There is no telling how many people in high places with incredible incomes were caught in his web of criminal activities. Death came to him in a New York City federal jail cell and must have been a relief for so many. An official autopsy listed suicide as the cause of death. I was talking telepathically to Joe one night and asked if he heard of Jeffrey Epstein. He said yes which was no surprise with all the news about him. Then I asked whether he was murdered in his cell as some suspect. He said yes again. My guess is the aliens watched him being suicided by using their ability to see into the past. Government officials never are likely to tell the truth.

Egypt

The Nefertiti bust either dates to the time when Nefertiti was queen of Egypt and later a Pharoah or it is a fake. Some German archaeologist claimed he dug up the bust in 1912. Today it is on display at an Egyptian museum in Berlin, Germany. As an icon of feminine beauty, it attracts more than half a million visitors annually. Experts in growing numbers, however, cast doubt on the authenticity of this bust. Paint, for example, looks very fresh for being buried in the ground over 3,000 years. Plaster covering a limestone base shows no signs of weathering or cracking. A YouTube program brought to light many more concerns. Joe showed up in this brightly lighted spaceship just after dark early in August of 2020. I asked him telepathically if the bust is a fake. He said yes by flashing his lights fast.

While I had his attention, I asked if aliens helped ancient Egyptians build the pyramids. He said yes by producing an amazing display of flashing white lights that reminded me of sparklers we lighted as kids on July 4. Are you sure about that? Another awesome round of flashing lights followed. No doubt the aliens have gone back into the past and watched the pyramids being built. His yes answer reminded me of the black and white avian humanoid picture I saw with the little grays and the same color painting that appeared on the wall of an Egyptian tomb in the computer. Perhaps these guys were the aliens who supplied all kinds of expertise for pyramid building. I mention this topic in the Flying chapter.

Sasquatch

They also are known as Bigfoot and Yeti. These guys seem like proto humans although they are not genetically related to any form of life on Earth according to an analysis of their genetic code. Sightings of them appear with increasing frequency in isolated parts of the U.S. and other areas all over the planet. They are tall and hairy beings said to weigh several hundred pounds. Everyone who has seen one agrees they are extremely powerful and potentially dangerous.

Joe and I have talked about them. He said aliens questioned some individuals by nonverbal telepathy. The Sasquatch said they are being sent from another planet. The aliens know from what planet they are coming, who is sending them here and for what reason. Assuming their numbers will increase rapidly, Joe and I agree there need to be laws, both state and federal, against hunting them down like wild game animals.

Phobos

It is one of two small moons surrounding Mars. The moon is oddly shaped and looks like a chunk of space rock captured by gravitational attraction. Some astronomers began to believe Phobos is an artificial satellite due to its rather strange characteristics. I asked Joe twice if it is an artificial satellite and his response both times was no. My guess is Phobos has been hollowed out and is being used as a military base and space port for cargo ships of considerable size unloading supplies including food for transfer to Mars. A similar situation surely applies to Deimos as well but on a substantially smaller scale.

Antarctica

Interesting stories about the frozen continent recently have been appearing in the news. Climate change, warming weather conditions and subglacial heat from volcanoes all are contributing to glacial melting. Huge tabular icebergs are calving off from continental glaciers helping to raise global sea level.

High-profile people are visiting Antarctica to see some amazing archaeology attractions, perhaps of alien origin, being kept secret for disturbing reasons. According to a YouTube program I watched during the summer of 2020, much was made of UFOs going to and coming from the continent along the western coast of South America. Credible information is lacking, and rumors run rampant. An alien base beneath the ice at the bottom of the world seemed highly unlikely to me.

I finally asked Joe if they really have a base down there. He said yes, they do.

The Moon

What a thrill it was for a geographer to see the Earth as it appears from the moon photographed by Apollo 11 astronauts on the lunar surface. After examining the photos in some detail, I began to wonder why the Earth seemed so small and far away. My feeling was the Earth should look a lot larger and closer based on the appearance of a full moon with so many visible craters. The same detail should apply to the Earth as seen from the moon.

Late in 1969 or early during 1970 aliens took me to see the Earth from their moon base. Why they bothered I wondered since the Apollo 11 photos already were so familiar to me. That was the problem they wanted to correct by letting me see the Earth for myself. I recall climbing up on top of something inside a dark moon base tunnel to look out a small window at ground level. The view was beyond overwhelming. It seemed magical and made a major impression on me. The Earth was illuminated by extremely bright sunlight. It looked enormous and so incredibly close to the moon that no open space appeared to separate the Earth and moon from my viewing angle down at the surface. Few geographic and physiographic features were visible.

Keep in mind our planet is roughly four times larger than the moon and 239,000 miles away on average. Only the Northern Hemisphere is visible above the horizon from their alien base north of the lunar equator. The Southern

Hemisphere is well below the horizon. A view of the entire planet as a completely round sphere is impossible to see from the surface like the Apollo 11 photos clearly show.

The Eurasian land mass was what I saw of the Northern Hemisphere. Due to a lack of atmosphere on the moon, extraordinarily brilliant sunlight reduces the appearance of all land areas to a dull tan rather than permitting a scene one might expect to see consisting of considerable color contrasts and shadings as on most world maps.

Photos and film clips of the lunar landscape taken by astronauts on the moon's surface sure seem so realistic, but there is a problem no one will notice unless they have been on the moon. Light is way too dim. It looks more like artificial light than blindingly bright sunlight. I have seen the real deal as a man in the moon. Pawning off phony lunar photos for people to peruse seemed perfectly safe to NASA.

Soon after the Apollo 11 astronauts returned from their historic moon landing, all kinds of articles and film clips began appearing in the computer claiming the Apollo mission was just an elaborate hoax.

The whole thing never happened. My response was don't confuse me with facts. Something, however. finally caught my attention. Evidence kept mounting astronauts on the moon were photographed in a movie studio well in advance of their landing. Especially interesting was some film footage of the flag flapping in a breeze on the lunar surface. NASA has had a tough time trying to create a convincing story to account for it.

Another problem difficult to explain was how crew members managed to survive high levels of radiation while passing twice through the Van Allan radiation belts surrounding the Earth. No radiation protection was provided due to weight constraints according to NASA which admitted it in public. Somehow it seems rather strange that the cabin crew were willing to tolerate excessive radiation exposure on their moon trip. But despite disturbing doubts, Apollo 11 served so successfully as a high-profile public project of a high-priced propaganda program for peaceful political purposes.

Fast-forward to 2019. NASA was celebrating the Apollo 11 moon landing fifty years earlier. All the publicity must have been enough to make my mind produce a mental image of the Earth as I saw it from the moon. The vision seemed like a long-forgotten dream after so many decades and made me wonder what to make of it. Joe showed up as usual after dark in his spaceship, so I asked him if he ever has been on the moon. He flashed his lights fast meaning yes. Then I asked whether the Earth is a lot larger and considerably closer to the moon than the NASA Earth photos show. He said yes again. I told him I knew because aliens showed me the Earth from their moon base. He already was aware of it much to my surprise. Lingering doubts finally disappeared. Joe and I have seen the Earth hanging huge above a lifeless lunar surface. It would be fantastic if other moon experiencers finally feel free to follow in my footsteps and favor us with some fascinating moon memories with aliens.

Joe appeared in his brightly lighted spaceship just beyond the border of my backyard during a wonderfully warm Spring night in 2020, and I began talking to him. My mind was full of disturbing doubts about Apollo 11. I decided to ask him if astronauts really did land on the moon. Joe would know for sure as an alien military officer. His flashing lights turned off and the rest drastically dimmed down. After several long seconds, all the lights came back on again. No was his answer. I asked the same question once more to make sure he understood my mental telepathy. His second response was the same as the first. Apollo 11 never landed on the moon. NASA had a very valid reason for deceiving the public with fake Earth and moon photos. This ought to be an enormous embarrassment for the space agency. The truth will be swept under the rug while deliberately duped taxpayers continue financing extremely expensive space programs for the benefit of NASA. As I continued talking to Joe, some slightly sickening strange shaky sensation suddenly started sinking swiftly into me.

After coming back inside, it occurred to me the moon-based aliens never said Apollo 11 was a hoax. Maybe they thought the dots would connect after seeing the Earth, but I had a hard time putting the pieces together. I cannot thank Joe enough for sharing some surprising space secrets with me.

I went outside to see Joe at dusk on August 31, 2020. The lights on his ship were flashing hello. We were having a Texas heat wave and the air temperature after sunset seemed sweltering. I decided to ask him just two quick questions and go back inside. Is it true that no Apollo astronaut ever has landed on the moon? He flashed a yes answer. Very possibly I may be the first human being to set foot on the moon rather than Neil Armstrong. Photos of astronauts on the moon collecting rock samples to bring back for NASA entered my mind. Modified Earth rocks probably were packed into carrying cases and placed onboard before the guys blasted off from Florida. Little wonder experts concluded the geology of the moon and Earth is amazingly similar. Informed space agency officials ought to be aware their priceless collection of moon rocks has no value.

Then I told Joe NASA is planning to land men on the moon in 2023 and begin building a lunar base. Are you military guys going to let them build one? His ship lights suddenly stopped flashing and dimmed down. No was the answer. Confrontation with aliens on the moon is possible and things may not pan out as planned. When news media discover something went wrong, they are going to have questions. NASA will be well prepared to present worthless weasel worded answers already attempting to discredit doubtful detractors while closely concealing conflict with aliens appearing armed. As so many say in ufology, the NASA acronym stands for Never A Straight Answer.

Mars

My boy scout troop was invited to visit an observatory after dark owned by the University of Cincinnati. An astronomer aimed the telescope at Mars and each of us took turns looking at the planet. Mars seemed surprisingly small, gray rather than red and out of focus. After that experience, I lost all interest in the planet.

Mars was making an unusually close approach to Earth in 2003. I told students in my geography class to go outside and see it after dark. Looking at the planet again was not my intention. Once was enough for me. When dinner and dishes were done, I changed my mind and decided to go see it a second time. Mars was barely visible just above the eastern horizon as a rather reddish point of light.

A fantastic emotional attraction suddenly swept over me while my attention was riveted on the planet. This extraordinary experience completely consumed me. Such a powerful feeling made no sense. My mind had hardly any active interest in Mars. Emotional involvement ended as soon as I walked across the front door threshold. It was over or so it seemed.

Nearly two decades later while outside talking to Joe at night, I suddenly asked him out of nowhere if he has been on Mars. Immediately I wondered where my mind was and why would I ask such a stupid question. Of course, there never would be any reason for him to go to Mars. Surely, he would say no. His lights flashed very fast meaning yes. So, I asked him if I have been on Mars. He said yes. More than once? He said yes again. Then I decided to ask a question that had been bothering me for years. Do I have friends on Mars? He said yes. I was completely bold-over and beside myself with joy. I must be the first human being to set foot on Mars beginning sometime during the 1940s.

Memory blocks placed on my Mars life experiences suddenly began to break open ever so slightly. I saw two little boys running through an underground tunnel to a spaceship hanging a couple feet above the floor. I was running faster than the Martian boy and arrived first at the ship. An opening appeared underneath the craft, and some guy standing close to the ship was going to help us up so we could look around inside. Even though I arrived first, he waited for the Martian boy and helped him before me. It was obvious the Martian boy was considered someone special. Friends went first when I was a boy at home.

A second vision of us together appeared later. We were sitting opposite one another at a small square table for two eating some treat in a bowl. A woman dressed in black was standing off to the side holding a big bowl of the treat to give us some more. It would be wonderful if the two of us could sit across from one another again at a small square table for two enjoying that tasty treat one last time.

My feeling is two other little Martian boys joined us as playmates sometime later. We grew up together and have been life-long friends.

Why the aliens selected me to play with these little guys remains a mystery. I have tried asking Joe several times if he knows, but either he has no information or more likely was told not to say. The answer probably is blocked in my memory. What makes sense is we share something in common with one another. Most likely all of us were hybridized with the same genetic material from an alien I call dad. He and I had a good relationship already as a kid. I would not be surprised if he took me to Mars to associate with his little boys. We were his family. The Martian boys probably got a big dose of alien intelligence genes which made them so special to the Martians as future leaders. I was their human contact to tell them about life on Earth and help them learn English. After

I penned this paragraph, Joe finally conceded the contents are correct.

During the summer of 2017, my mind started receiving printed text messages and handwritten notes in a complex language that was unfamiliar to me. To make a long story short, I realized after a while my Martian friends were trying to contact me and knew I was fluent in their language. Contact finally stopped once they realized my ability to understand their language was blocked so I never responded to their correspondence.

The written Martian language looks peculiar. They have more letters in their alphabet than in English. All letters have most peculiar shapes. Writing is right justified or goes from right to left rather than left to right. Only lower-case letters are used. There is no spacing between words and one sentence is not separated from the next. Messages look like one extremely long line of connected letters.

Most likely I learned the Martian language after being with my friends for so many years. There is, however, another possibility. I went to Mars for several weeks or a month at a time to be taught the language. That would seem impossible. My family would wonder what happened to me and there would be all kinds of investigations and searches. But it works because of alien time reversal. This sounds like something straight out of science fiction although it is for real. Here is how it works.

A tractor light beam from a spaceship lifts me out of bed during the dead of night. An alarm clock in my bedroom shows 3:15 AM. I am taken to Mars for a month on a ship going faster than the speed of light according to Joe. Then the ship brings me home and beams me back to bed. The alarm clock now shows 3:30 AM. I have been gone for 15 minutes. I was taken into the future for a month and then returned to the past which is now the present. My hair and nails grew while I was gone for a month but when I return, they remain the exact same length as when I left home. Life goes on as usual. No one will know what really went on with me.

I ended up asking Joe two more Mars questions later while talking with him outside one night. I wanted to know if he told them something about my grandson Jon and me. He said yes. Do they speak English with a slight accent? His remarkable response was a spectacular show of colorful flashing lights. He said yes and was so surprised I knew. Obviously, Joe had no idea they telepathically told me something from Mars. If you wonder about the real reason for his recent military meeting with Martians, consider the contents of Chapter 13 as clues.

Grays on Mars must surely seem surprising. The truth is they own the Red Planet and all its inhabitants. Protection is provided as well as some food and supplies. Anyone planning a permanent Mars base would be well advised to acquire permission first or face considerable alien confrontation.

I asked Joe twice if they have a base in the asteroid blet on Ceres. He said yes both times. Then I told him about photos taken on Mars of a rectangular object that leaves tractor trails in the soil. Some similar sort of object has been photographed on Pluto making tractor snow tracks. I asked if they have a base on Pluto. He said yes. No telling how many other bases and satellite stations they already maintain throughout the solar system which must be under their control. I wonder whether NASA and the pentagon have any idea just how powerful this alien group is. Recent congressional hearings on UAPs or UFOs confirm no government official with access to classified information intends to admit in public these objects are alien spaceships coming here from light years away. The piece de resistance grays covet most is planet Earth and they are planning to possess it.

My dad came to visit with me at home not very long ago. His concerns seemed centered on completing final preparations for an impending alien invasion.

CHAPTER 13

INVASION

Astronomers observe a cluster of objects passing through our solar system in the outer reaches. Experts conclude the cluster probably consists of artificial objects. No one seems concerned since the cluster is so far away and a trajectory is difficult to determine. Once these objects reach the inner solar system, all now agree this is a fleet of alien spaceships. The fleet disappears magically near Mars and cannot be found. Nothing is said officially to prevent public panic, but those in the know are more than a little disturbed.

Suddenly the fleet appears once again on optical and radio telescopes as well as special military surveillance monitors just 5,000 miles from Earth. There are 100 ships in the fleet and each one is larger than an aircraft carrier. No doubt they contain an enormous amount of military equipment and personnel.

Ships descend into a polar orbit forming a tight ring around the planet some 1,000 miles away. The United Nations General Assembly meets in an emergency session. A decision is made to contact the aliens. Their message is cobbled together quickly and transmitted in several different languages. No response is received. Military preparedness in the U.S. is upgraded to DEFCON 3.

Mother ships drop way down to 10,000 feet and open their wide bay doors. Thousands of small spaceships are released which quickly spread across the globe and position themselves over every major metropolitan area. Their hostile intent becomes evident to everyone.

Governments scramble jet fighters to engage the enemy ships. They are no match for such highly advanced military craft surrounded by impenetrable force fields. Planes are pulverized by particle beams or plummet to the ground and explode after electric power is blocked. Invaders take control of all open-air space in practically no time.

Urban infrastructures now become easy targets for destruction. Power plants and electric grids are wiped out. All forms of communication including satellites are eliminated. Water supplies and pumping plants are removed suddenly from service. Basic life support systems swiftly disappear.

People soon panic and flee from cities. Roads and expressways become completely congested with vehicles leaving town. Death rates rise rapidly among those remaining at home. Troops are rushed to rural areas and advised to live off the land as they prepare to enter asymmetric engagements against enemy attackers.

You know by now just how this show ends. Hollywood suddenly hurries to help save humanity. Small squads of freedom fighters and military men hiding in hinterland isolation decisively defeat our alien invaders. The planet is saved, and survivors live happily ever after. Who'da thunk it!

Be of good cheer. No alien fleet is lurking in the outer fringes of our solar system. Truth is human beings are destroying this planet without any alien assistance. Inhabitants of planets in other galaxy solar systems say they have no interest in stopping us. According to them, our section of the galaxy is full of dead planets destroyed by civilizations at our level of development. We are descending along a perilous path to a tipping point from which there is no return.

Grays **constitute** the most powerful group of alien residents on this planet. How long they have been here is not known, but for some lengthy time is likely. Their spaceships are equipped with highly advanced propulsion systems and weapons. Security on their twin planet Terra between the Earth and Venus in another dimension of the solar system is tight suggesting it could be one big military base. My feeling is other resident alien groups like the Pleiadeans certainly cannot compete against them.

Grays and their hybrids have collected all kinds of information about us for decades. This material is stored in considerably complex computers for instant retrieval. They always can obtain any data needed no matter how restricted or secret. This includes the nuclear missile launch codes held for the President in the white house or wherever he travels regardless of how often the codes are changed. Top secret information generated by government, industry and research facilities is known to them. Nuclear missile bases have been penetrated and aliens know how to start and stop launch sequences. They can open any bank vault door without detection or invisibly penetrate right through them. Funds in every bank account can be transferred electronically to their own account without leaving a trace. Large pension funds probably have lost millions of dollars and never realized it. I mention all this because the grays are very well informed about everything and must be ready to invade.

An elegant argument heard frequently these days is aliens will nor invade because they could have done so long ago if they had any interest. It is a line of logic that once made sense to me. I saw the light after talking with the hybrids. Their thinking is aliens have no interest in invading underdeveloped planets. What they want is a world like ours that is fully developed and scientifically advanced with plenty of resources to exploit. We are a plum ripe for the picking.

Likely targets during an invasion already are apparent in news media. A background in military geography is not needed to identify the dots and connect them. I will give you an idea what to watch for as a geographer with some of my own observations.

The key to recognizing targets is a sudden and substantial interruption of one or more necessary public services in a single country or extending even worldwide in scope. Such an event caught my attention when power outages in major metropolitan areas across the U.S. occurred simultaneously on April 27, 2017. Strangely enough, no two locations had the same problem. All were due to different kinds of mechanical failures rather than a computer attack on the national power grid. The probability of this happening by mere chance alone is astronomically small. Only aliens can orchestrate all outages at once whenever they want. This was just a dry run prior to a major military movement when power disruption is essential.

Stay with me for a minute while I name the power failure locations. They included San Diego, Los Angeles, San Francisco, Seattle, Salt Lake City, Phoenix and Tucson, Chicago extending up Lake Michigan, Ohio River Valley, the entire East Coast, Florida along the Gulf Coast to Houston and north up to Dallas. A map published by the National UFO Center shows areas with the greatest number of UFO sightings. It fits exactly over these same urban areas. There is little doubt where aliens have the greatest interest for some special sort of military action.

Telephone service went out repeatedly in 2018 for varying lengths of time. Phone outages occurred nationally for AT&T, Spectrum and Verizon. AT&T cellphone service went out twice in the same location on November 15, 2017, and November 15, 2018. Hard to believe this was just a coincidence. Out in my Hill Country area of Texas already under alien control, all phone service was interrupted for 14 hours on June 27, 2019. The length of time was unprecedented. No one at the phone cooperative could confirm any cause. Amazon lost contact with customers nationally as well as Europe and the Middle East. Singapore suddenly lost almost all electric service. This city has a strategic location at the eastern entrance to the Strait of Malacca with control over significant world shipping lanes. Several large banks suddenly lost contact with their customers and the same thing happened to Costco. Keep a list of such failures for future reference. They are starting to display a disturbing pattern.

Dr. David Jacobs and Timothy Good both are convinced the goal of the grays is planet acquisition. My hybrid family member Joe who is in a military position to know for sure says yes whenever I ask if they are going to invade us. Experiences on the inside convince me yes is correct. Grays have been busy breeding and training their hybrids for decades to invade and control this planet. A contact of mine told me recently some relative who once worked at Area 51 with the grays said their plan is to invade the largest countries first. Once they are under control, remaining smaller countries are expected to surrender in a final domino collapse of world governments.

This invasion was planned by professionals for execution by experts. Large fleets of lighted spaceships are slated to show up soon after sunset followed by blazing blitzkrieg attacks without any warning during the dead of night. Game over becomes apparent barely after bombing action begins with alarming death and destruction

Government officials and scientists with distinguished degrees, who take pride in their total ignorance of gray intentions, have a hard time believing these aliens already are invading. Top military officers, who have no interest in locating and removing numerous gray bases, now are clueless how to defend this country against thousands of invading ships invisible even on advanced radar screens. Deep Underground Military Bases, or DUMBs, fill up quickly with all kinds of high-profile elite while "the little people" are left to fend for themselves. Aliens have acoustic weapons capable of collapsing substantial subterranean structures and tunnels. Survivors, if any, are going to have a hard time finding their way out in the dark through all the dirt, debris, and dead bodies.

At the NORAD base well within Cheyenne Mountain in Colorado, there is a labyrinth of large tunnels. No doubt aliens already are aware how to destroy them. If they decide instead to occupy the base, they can drive directly through the tightly locked blast doors and eliminate all personnel.

Folks tend to be well armed in this country. I read recently there are six guns for every resident here in Texas. Guns will be like bows and arrows against rifles. Unlike rifles, however, captured alien weapons will not work without immediately inserting an activation code. We are so far behind the curve in science and technology there is no hope of prevailing against these invaders. Freedom fighters and military men hiding in hinterland locations will not last long enough to decisively defeat the alien attackers. So much for Hollywood coming to the rescue. The next paragraph contains disturbing content difficult to consider. Maybe open minds might manage to benefit from it.

Hybrid military officers look human like us, but they have a superior alien intelligence and science fiction weapons. Some security officer once showed me a small handgun that shoots bullets of compressed energy at such a high velocity they can rip right through the human body and leave entry and exit holes the diameter of dimes. Officers are marvelous mind readers. One of them reading your mind knows you intend to shoot so he opens fire first. Names and addresses along with any additional information can be accessed mentally. These guys see into the future and can watch an attach before it begins. They also see into the past and can watch attacks after they have happened. When they make themselves invisible, attacks are possible without any warning. They are experts at mind control. Once under their mental influence, resistance is impossible. Aggression against them will result in severely shortened life spans. Anyone who opposes them will be "eliminated." There are no plans for taking prisoners. Game over becomes apparent barely after troops arrive with alarming death and destruction.

Aliens have no interest in laying waste to this planet. A fully functioning world would be beneficial to them. Damage is bound to be limited. Infrastructure integrity is intended. Stay safe inside and avoid action outside. Panic is pointless and probably will prolong the problem.

CHAPTER 14

FINALE

A low-level cloud cover made the night sky seem somewhat dismal while departing Eagle Pass after class for home a hundred miles away. Highway 57 heading out or town arrives in La Pryor, Texas, 46 miles later passing through a desolate area of uninhabited rangeland dominated by desert plants and stands of stunted woody vegetation adapted to high heat and reduced rainfall. Driving through this lonesome country alone in the dark, I decided to keep my mind active and alert by thinking about how to handle dead body disposal during an alien invasion. Funeral directors surely would have a hard time collecting enough caskets to stuff their stiffs. A substantial supply shortage could cause casket prices to increase almost instantly. Cremation takes considerable time and dead bodies decaying on long waiting lists signals some significant sanitation situation soon should surface.

A large deer standing on the highway right-of-way showed up suddenly in my high beam headlights. I reduced speed rapidly to head off having it hanging from the front bumper. The doe never moved a muscle as if in a state of suspended animation. While I watched it, something very strange happened. First a fine mist formed and finished off the head. The remaining carcass then was rapidly consumed. Hair and hide vaporized and vanished after several amazing seconds.

I finally realized security officers following me home in their overhead spaceship were reading my mind and wanted to show how they handle waste disposal with their hi-tech equipment. In case you failed to see the significance of such a show, let me lend a little assistance. The doe still was standing and alive although paralyzed when vaporized by them. The thought crossed my mind aliens certainly could use this type of disposal device on perfectly paralyzed humans.

Alien planners probably project a death rate like other planets they already have invaded. Human remains will be vaporized in a speedy and sanitary manner. My Malthusian mind makes me wonder whether worldwide population reduction will result in a better balance between food production and consumption.

As an alien-controlled country, vaporization becomes the new normal now for dead body disposal. Demand dramatically decreases for pricey cemetery plots. Once gramps dies and departs to his last destination for reincarnation, just load him onto some set of wheels and drive down to the nearest vaporization station. Personnel are prepared to process him professionally for pennies per pound on a dead weight basis. Frequent financial fraud for fancy family funerals finally folds forever.

EPILOGUE

After reading all my alien material, either doubt or denial must represent your reaction. Dealing with doubt and denial is difficult, but fortunately times and tides are turning for the better. National news reports reveal an influential individual put pressure on pentagon personnel to admit UFOs are real rather than "psychological aberrations" postulated by psychologists. A recently disseminated pentagon document never divulged UFOs are spaceships armed with awesome weapons against which adequate defense appears doubtful at best. I imagine many more surprising secrets also await selective sanitizing during disclosure. Aliens could take control of all open-air over North America with alarming ease. Secrets considered sensational have no hope of publication to prevent total panic. Both my books deliberately avoid describing actual disconcerting accounts as an attempt at allaying any abiding angst about aliens.

Considerable concern concentrates on whether anyone imagines an impending alien invasion already is approved. I have tried to talk with Joe about it. As a high-ranking alien military officer, he is well informed. Invasion is certain with no interest in consequences. His talents and training seem better suited to combat and control rather than helping hapless humans. Open minds ought to start stockpiling supplies before a need arises. Closed minds opting to open once attacks are in progress is probably too little too late.

Now is the time to admit an alien presence already prevails among us. When their plans for this planet finally are activated, a radical new reality will result while the world as we know it comes to an end.

www.ingramcontent.com/pod-product-compliance
Lightning Source LLC
Chambersburg PA
CBHW051234210726
48290CB00003B/949